Ragged Bear's
Book of Stories

For Leah, Georgie and Phoebe

Diz

First published in the United Kingdom in 1999 by Ragged Bears Publishing Limited,
Milborne Wick, Sherborne, Dorset DT9 4PW

Distributed by Ragged Bears Limited, Ragged Appleshaw, Andover, Hampshire SP11 9HX
Tel: 01264 772269
Text and illustrations copyright © 1999 by Diz Wallis

A CIP record of this book is available from the British Library

ISBN 1 85714 188 1

Printed in China

Ragged Bear's
Book of Stories

17 Classic Stories for Children
retold and illustrated by
Diz Wallis

Ragged Bears Publishing

 Contents

The Elves
and the Shoemaker

It had not been a good week, or month, or year, come to that. The shoemaker had been ill and although he was better now he was still very tired and felt too frail to work. "This is all we have left in the world," he said to his wife, showing her one small coin. "It's scarcely enough to buy us a loaf of bread. There is only enough leather left to make one small pair of shoes. What will become of us?"

"Something will turn up," said his wife, trying to comfort him. "Cut out the leather now, we can start to stitch the shoes in the morning."

"Whatever you say, my dear, whatever you say." And he did as she said right away. He cut out the leather and went up to bed. Although they hardly slept at all for worry.

However, in the morning when the couple came downstairs, instead of leather pieces laid out upon the bench they found the most perfectly made pair of shoes. "We must be imagining things," said the shoemaker. He closed his eyes and rubbed them, and his wife rubbed hers but the shoes were still there.

"It must be magic," he said.

"Little folk more like," replied his wife.

They were still marvelling about it when the door of the shop opened and in came a customer. "Ah," said she, "those look like just the shoes for me, small enough to fit my little feet. They look so perfect, they look so neat." And she tried them on. They really did look as though they had been made for her. She was so pleased, she gave the shoemaker far more than he would have dared to ask. Then she left the shop leaving the shoemaker holding enough money in his hand to buy leather for two pairs of shoes and a little left over besides.

"If you cut the pieces large," said his wife that evening, "we can ask more money for them."

"What ever you say, my dear, what ever you say." And he did what she told him, right away. He cut out the pieces and left them on his work bench, just as he had done the night before. Then the couple went to bed feeling puzzled but pleased and hoping that the same wonderful thing would happen again.

Sure enough, the next morning, two more beautifully stitched pairs of shoes stood upon the bench where the leather had been. But before the shoemaker and his wife had had a chance to remark upon it, the door of the shop opened and in came another customer. "Ah!" said he, "Just what I'm looking for. A pair of shoes that are big and broad and so finely stitched they must not be ignored. If they fit me I'll take them and the other pair too." He tried them on and they really did look as though they had been made for him. He was so pleased that he paid far more than the shoemaker would have dared to ask, then left the shop.

The shoemaker now had enough money in his hand to buy leather for four pairs of shoes and a little left over besides. Each night he left the leather cut out, and each morning he found the pieces made into shoes, and there was never any shortage of customers. Things went on this way for some time and the couple grew quite wealthy. "I think it's time, we ought," said his wife at last, "to find out who it is who's been helping us. Let's leave a candle alight upon the bench tonight. We can hide behind this curtain and watch."

That evening, as the light began to fade, they lit the candle. Then they hid behind the curtain and waited. They waited and waited. In the corner a clock ticked and tocked. The couple were growing tired, the candle burning low. They had almost given up when the clock struck twelve. From somewhere near the door there came a tiny scratching and the sound of little feet upon the floor.

Two tiny, ragged men appeared, with wild red hair and straggly beards. They scrambled up on to the bench and started at once to work. Their needles flashed to and fro so fast the shoemaker and his wife were amazed. It took five minutes for those little elves to do work that would have taken the old man weeks to complete. When they had finished the little fellows hopped off the bench and away.

"Such kindness deserves a reward," said his wife.

"Let's make them some fine clothes and give them some food, for I've never seen little folk before so ragged and shabby and thin."

"Whatever you say, my dear, whatever you say." And he did what she said, but not right away for it was very late and they were tired.

In the morning they set about their task. He went into the workshop and took the softest leather he could find and made two pairs of teeny, tiny shoes. She went to her work-box and sorted out wisps of lace and snippets of silk, and sewed them into clothes fit for very small gentlemen. When their work was finished, they lay their gifts on the bench along with a bowl of porridge.

As the clock struck twelve, in came the little men just as before. They scrambled up on to the bench and looked around. But instead of finding leather to stitch, they found their clothes and a good round meal. They dressed and ate and danced and sang. They sang in the smallest voices you ever heard. But behind their curtain, the cobbler and his wife caught every word.

"Once we were poor boys, ragged and thin,
Our fingers were raw, boys, from hard sewing,
But now we are dressed like fine gentlemen,
We never need stitch, boys, nor cobble again."

Then they hopped off the table and out into the night, laughing and singing all the way. No one ever saw the elves again. But with their help the shoemaker and his wife had grown so prosperous they could manage very well on their own.

And for the rest of their long lives the couple enjoyed the best of health and always seemed to have good luck.

The Three Wishes

"Where's the firewood?" said the old woman to her husband.

"Well, dear," said he, "it was like this. I went to the wood like you said and I was just going to chop down a tree, when I heard a teeney, weeney voice telling me to stop. Well I looked all round but I couldn't see a soul. So I lifted my axe and was about to swing it when I heard the teeney, weeney voice again. Well, I looked down and there stood a tiny fairy. He said to me, 'Stop! Don't chop! This here tree's my little home.'

"'Well,' says I, 'I won't, Sir. I wouldn't chop your home down for all the world.' Well the fairy he was so grateful, he gave me three wishes. But he said I must be careful not to waste them; wishes are like water in a sieve!"

"Quite right, husband," said the old woman, "such good luck doesn't happen to the likes of us too often. We must be very careful indeed."

Now, the old man felt very hungry - "What's for dinner?" he asked. "Nothing," said the old woman, "the cupboard's quite bare. But with those wishes, we'll be eating like kings for the rest of our lives."

The old man was famished. "Oh I wish," said he, almost without thinking, "that I had a string of big, fat sausages to eat!" No sooner had he said this, than a string of sausages fell down the sooty chimney and into the grate.

His wife was furious. "Fool!" she cried, "How could you be so careless? That's one wish, wasted and gone, and all upon a string of sausages too! Why, I wish they'd jump up and stick onto your stupid nose!" Then she clapped her hand across her mouth, but it was too late, the words were already out.

The sausages leapt out of the grate and attached themselves to the end of the old man's nose.

"Silly old woman, look what you've done. That's another wish wasted and gone!"

"Oh dear!" said the old woman, "Whatever shall we do, we've only one wish left."

She looked at the old man, he did look very odd with the string of big fat sausages hanging from his nose! "Pull them off, wife," he said, "and don't say another word."

She got up from the table and pulled at the string of sausages. She pulled and pulled but they just would not shift. "Harder!" said the old man. And she heaved and heaved and heaved until she felt quite overwhelmed and had to sit down.

It seemed the sausages were part of the old man's nose. He could wear them wound up and tied in a bow. The old woman tried to picture going to church on Sunday, the congregation laughing. The humiliation was too much to bear!

"Oh I wish those stupid sausages would go back where they came from!" Then she drew in her breath as if to suck the words right back. But it was too late. The sausages had fallen off and already disappeared back up the sooty chimney, where they came from.

The old couple sat a while and looked at each other. Then they said, "Wishes are too tricky for simple folk like us. Oh, what fools we were. We had three wishes and we wasted them all!"

"And," muttered the old man, sadly to himself, "I could have done with those sausages too!"

The Little Red Hen

Every day the little red hen would scratch around the farmyard and peck up the scraps and grain that had been scattered round for her. One day she found a small pile of corn that had escaped through a hole in one of the sacks in the barn. She put her head on one side and thought, "There's enough here to grow a little crop."

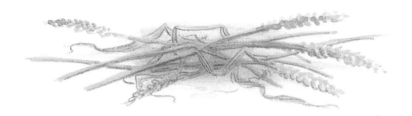

So she gathered it up and went to ask her friends for help. The pig and rat and tabby-cat all sat dozing in the soft sunshine.

She said, "Who will help me sow this corn?"

"Not I," grunted the pig.

"Not I," squeaked the rat.

"Not I," purred the sleepy tabby-cat.

So the little red hen had to sow the corn all by herself. When it had grown high and was the colour of gold, she knew it was ripe and ready to cut. So she went to her friends to ask for their help.

She said, "Who'll help me cut the corn?"

"Not I," grunted the pig.

"Not I," squeaked the rat.

"Not I," purred the sleepy tabby-cat.

So the little red hen had to cut the corn all by herself. She shook the stalks and gathered up the grain. She knew that grain must go to the miller to be ground, so she went to her friends to ask them for their help.

She said, "Who'll help me take this grain to the miller?"

"Not I," grunted the pig.

"Not I," squeaked the rat.

"Not I," purred the sleepy tabby-cat.

So the little red hen took the grain to the miller all by herself. She came back with a bag of fine white flour. It was time to take the flour to the baker to be baked into bread. So the little red hen went to her friends to ask for help.

She said, "Who'll help me take this flour to the baker?"

"Not I," grunted the pig.

"Not I," squeaked the rat.

"Not I," purred the sleepy tabby-cat.

So the little red hen took the bag of flour to the baker, all by herself. The flour was made into dough. The dough was shaped into a loaf, which was put into an oven to bake. When the loaf came out it was crusty and brown and it smelt wonderful! The little red hen carried it back to the farm.

Her friends came to meet her.

She said "Who'll help me eat this crusty brown bread?"

"I will," grunted the pig.

"I will," squeaked the rat.

"I will," purred the cat who was not sleepy anymore.

"No you won't," said the little red hen, "I'll eat it all by myself!"

And do you know, that is exactly what she did!

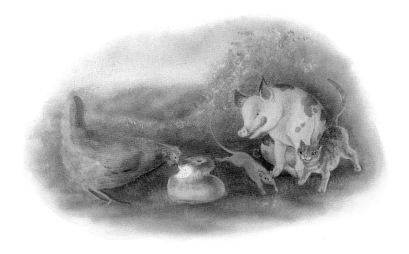

The Tortoise and the Hare

One fine day, old tortoise was walking down the lane, when he heard somebody laughing and looked round. There stood a hare, and she was mocking him for being so slow. "Hey, old dodderer, old plodderer where are you going? I don't think you'll ever get there at that pace!"

"Madam," said the tortoise, very slowly, "as I always say, more haste: less speed! A tortoise always gets to where he's going in time. Would you care to have a race?"

"As you wish," said the hare, "if you're sure you can make it. I don't want you to tire yourself out!" And she laughed and laughed. In fact, she laughed so much she thought her sides might split!

The animals agreed where the winning line should be, a mile or so away across some fields and down a twisty lane to the stream.

"On your marks. Get set. Go," said the tortoise very slowly.

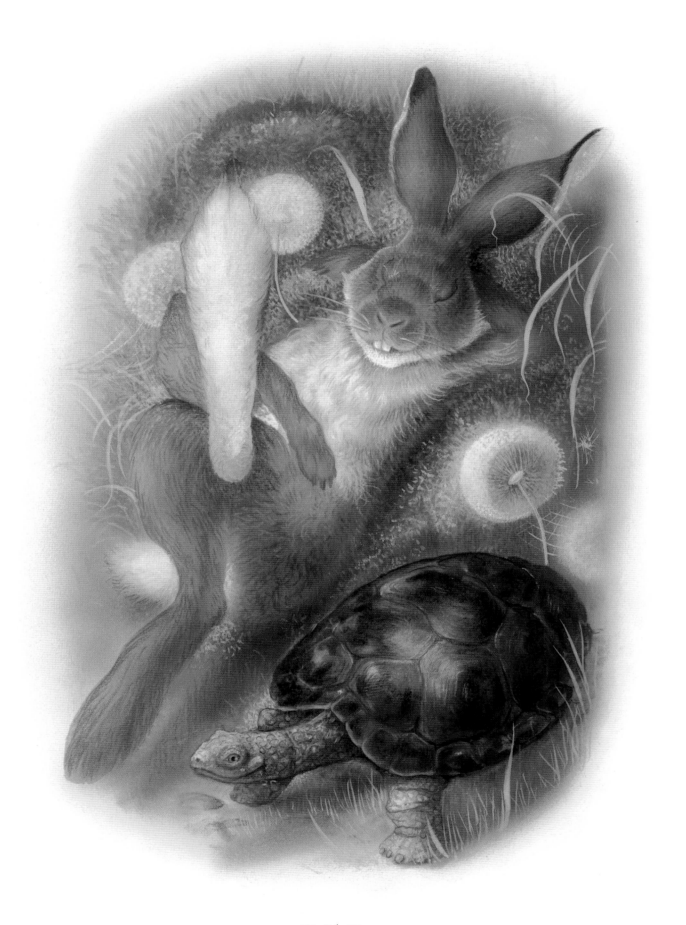

The hare was off in a flash with a leap and a bound. Over hillock, over tussock she flew. The tortoise plodded off towards his goal.

The sun was high and hot and the hare thought, "I could rest and have a nap. It'll be hours before he gets here and I'm already nearly at the finishing line."

So she shut her eyes and dozed in the dreamy afternoon, as the tortoise plodded slowly on toward his goal.

The sun was going down before the hare awoke. She opened her eyes and looked around. "There's nobody in sight. He probably hasn't even started yet. But I'd better get a move on just the same." Away she raced again. It was not far to go now, only down the twisty lane to the brook.

Imagine her surprise when she turned the final twist, just in time to see the tortoise reach the stream. "See what I mean?" said the tortoise to the puffing hare, "I overtook you an hour ago. Slow and easy does it every time!"

Sleeping Beauty
or
Briar-Rose

In a kingdom far away, there lived a King and Queen who longed, above all things, for a daughter. One day, while the Queen was bathing in a pool, a frog hopped up onto the bank and spoke to her, "Before the year has passed, you shall have the daughter you so desire."

Sure enough, before the year was over, the couple had a beautiful baby girl. They named her Briar-Rose. A great banquet was thrown to celebrate her birth and all the fairies in the Kingdom were to be invited, for it was known they would bestow blessings upon the child. Now, the problem was, the King only had twelve golden dinner plates and there were thirteen fairies in the land. What was he to do? One of the fairies was old and nasty and had not been seen for many years, so she was not sent an invitation.

The party began and one by one the fairies went over to the baby's cradle and blessed her with gifts such as beauty and kindness and sweetness of voice and wisdom. Just as the eleventh fairy had given her blessing, the doors of the palace burst open and in flew the thirteenth fairy in a fury of spite, because she had not been asked to the feast.

She went straight to the side of the cradle and cursed the child, saying that in her fifteenth year she would prick her finger on a spindle and drop down dead! Then she left without another word.

The party fell silent in horror. The Queen began to sob, but the twelfth fairy had not yet given her gift. She stepped forward and said, "Your majesties, be comforted, for although I cannot undo the spell, I can soften it. Instead of dying, the princess, and all around her, will fall into a deep sleep, for one hundred years.

When that time is up a prince will come and awaken her with a kiss."

The King and Queen were desperate to alter the child's fate. So they ordered that all the spinning wheels and spindles in the land be burned on a great bonfire. The flames of this fire, it is said, could be seen for miles and it burned for weeks. There was not a single spinning wheel or spindle left in the kingdom. Or so it seemed.

The princess grew up just as the fairies had promised. She had beauty and wisdom and sweetness. Everybody loved her.

On her fifteenth birthday, whilst the King and Queen were away, Briar-Rose had been left alone in the palace; she did not mind for she was able to explore. An old palace like that was full of passages and rooms and turrets, where no one ever went. So the princess wandered round. At last she found a staircase that wound up and up. The steps were worn away and dusty. They had not been used for years. A very odd humming noise was coming from behind a little door at the top.

She pushed the door aside and saw an old woman sitting at a strange machine. The princess had never seen anything like it. "What are you doing?" she asked. "Why!" said the old woman, who was really the thirteenth fairy, "I'm spinning at my spinning wheel. Why not come in and try it for yourself?"

The Princess was fascinated and sat down at the wheel. The moment she had the spindle in her hand, the magic began to work. She pricked her finger on it and at once fell into the deepest sleep.

So too did the whole household, and the King and Queen, for they had just returned. Courtiers and guards fell asleep where they stood. Horses fell asleep in the stables, pigeons on the roof. The cats and dogs began to dream. In the kitchen the maid stopped plucking the hen, the cook stopped scolding the scullery boy, and both nodded off. The spit stopped turning, the fire stopped burning and even the very flies on the walls stopped their droning and slept.

A great, tangled thorn hedge sprang up around the palace, completely enclosing it.

Rumour of the curse that had befallen the household spread quickly. And the princes came from far and wide, to try their luck at rescuing the sleeping beauty. Many tried; all failed. They were torn to shreds on the terrible thorns.

But, one day, after a long, long time, a prince passed by this wall of thorns and he asked an old man he met, what lay behind it. As soon as he heard the tale of the lost palace and beautiful Briar-Rose, he determined to cut his way through to save her. He set about his task at once. He lifted his sword to strike at the first cruel stem and as he did so, a strange thing happened. The thorns turned into white flowers and the hedge parted, making a pathway right to the palace. The spell was lifting.

All he could hear was silence, in the dusty rooms and corridors. No dog arose to bark at him, no guard lifted a sword to stop him.

It was just as he had been told. The whole household was asleep. At last he found the staircase to the turret where Briar-Rose slept. She lay on the bed where the twelfth fairy had placed her exactly one hundred years before. And she was truly beautiful.

The prince leant over and kissed her. At once she awoke. Then the flies on the walls began to buzz, the fire sprang up, the spit turned, the maid began to pluck the hen, the cook scolded the scullery boy, the dogs barked, the cats purred, the pigeons flew off the roof, and the horses neighed. Guards, courtiers, King and Queen all stretched themselves and yawned.

The whole palace was awake and ready to celebrate.

In due course, the prince and Briar-Rose married and lived happily together till the end of their days.

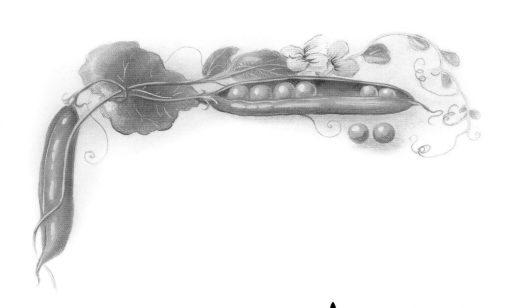

The Princess and the Pea

There was once a prince who wanted to marry, but no ordinary princess would do for him. His princess had to be one of the most noble birth, the most delicate beauty, and of the most fragile and sensitive nature. He searched the whole world over. Princesses he found by the score, but how could he tell which was the right one? In the end he gave up and came home to his mother and father.

One night there was the most dreadful storm. The lightning flashed, the thunder crashed and the torrents of rain lashed the castle walls. Now and again there was a lull in the tempest and it was during one of these that someone was heard beating at the door. It was opened and in fell a girl soaked to the skin, and battered and bedraggled by the storm. She said she was a princess, though this was hard to believe. Certainly she was beautiful but what a state she was in. Her wet clothes clung to her like so many rags. Her hair hung down around her like strings. Still she insisted she was indeed, truly a princess, and of the finest pedigree too.

"Huff!" said the ageing Queen to herself, "We'll see about that! I'll put her to the test! If she fails it, we'll know she's an imposter. If she passes, well..." She invited the girl to spend the night in a certain bed that was much, much higher than normal. Onto the mattress she placed a pea, then she covered this with piles of other mattresses and quilts, till the girl had to use a ladder to climb into the bed and was forced to sleep with her head almost touching the ceiling.

The next morning at breakfast the old Queen asked the princess if she had slept well. "Oh no!" said the girl, "I didn't sleep a wink. I tossed and turned the whole night through. There was something in that bed that felt like a rock and I'm bruised all over, black and blue! Oh! What torture it was!"

"That settles it," declared the Queen. "This is the princess," she said to her son, "that you have been looking for. For only a real princess of the highest birth, and of the most delicate and sensitive type, would ever have been disturbed by such a tiny, little pea underneath all those mattresses, at night!"

Molly Whuppie

Many years ago, there lived a poor wood cutter and his wife. They had so many children that they could not feed them all. So they took the three youngest girls and left them in a wood, to fend for themselves.

The girls walked all day until darkness fell. They were tired and hungry and cold. So when Molly, who was the youngest, saw a light flicker in the distance, it shone like a ray of hope. As they drew nearer they saw it came from a house. They knocked on the door.

"What do you want?" said the woman who opened it.

"Some food, please," they begged, "and a bed for the night."

"Oh no!," said the woman, "I can't let you in. My husband's a giant. If he comes home and finds you here, he'll chop you into little bits!" But the girls pleaded and promised they would leave before he returned. They looked so desperate she could not refuse.

Now, the girls had scarcely begun to eat when the giant came home. "What's this?" he roared as he looked at the visitors. His wife begged him not hurt them. "They're cold and tired and hungry and they're leaving right away," she said.

"No! They shall stay the night," declared the giant. No one dared say any more about it.

Now, the giant had three daughters of his own, and Molly and her sisters were to share their bed. Before they went to sleep, the giant said he had some presents for them. Round the necks of his own girls he placed gold chains, whilst round the necks of his guests he placed straw ropes. Molly noticed this and decided she would do well to stay awake.

As soon as the others were soundly asleep, she swapped the chains and ropes around. Now it was Molly and her sisters, who wore the gold chains and the giant's own girls who wore the straw ropes. It was a very clever move, as you shall see.

In the middle of the night, when all the house was black as pitch, the giant came into their room. He groped in the darkness for the straw ropes. Then he lifted the owners up out of bed and biffed them with his cudgel, never guessing they were his own dear girls. Then he went back to bed very pleased with himself!

"So!" thought Molly. "That's what giants are like." Then she woke her sisters, and quickly and quietly away they ran.

They ran and ran without stopping until they reached the King's castle. Molly asked to see him and she told her tale. The King was pleased because he did not like the giant. "Molly Whuppie," he said, "you're a brave, bold girl and have done very well. If you would do better, go back again and steal the sword that hangs above the giant's bed. I shall marry my first son to your eldest sister." Molly thought this would be very good fortune indeed, so she agreed to try.

She crept back into the giant's house without being noticed and hid beneath his bed. The giant came home in the evening, ate a huge supper and went to bed. He was soon snoring loudly. Molly slipped out and took down the sword, but the sword rattled in its scabbard and the giant leapt up. Molly was off at a fair trot with the giant chasing after her. She ran until she reached the Hair's Breadth Bridge. She got across but the giant could not follow. He stopped and shook his fist at her. "Molly Whuppie," he roared until the ground shook beneath their feet, "woe betide you, if you come back here again."

"Oh! How you scare me, I wouldn't dare me come back again, except twice more!" cried Molly from the other side.

The King was pleased with the sword for he detested the giant. "Molly Whuppie," he said, "you're a brave, bold girl and have done very well. If you would do better, go back again to the giant's house and steal the purse from beneath his pillow. I will marry my second son to your middle sister." Molly thought this would be good fortune indeed so she agreed to try.

She returned, as before, to the giant's house and hid beneath his bed. She waited until he was snoring loudly then she slipped out and pulled the purse from beneath his pillow. Just as she was leaving the coins in the purse jangled and the giant leapt up. He was furious. They ran and they ran until they reached the Hair's Breadth Bridge. Molly got across but the giant could not follow. He stood and shook his fist at her. "Molly Whuppie," he roared until the ground shook beneath their feet, "woe betide you if you ever come back here again!"

Molly called back from the other side, "Oh! how you scare me, I wouldn't dare me ever return but once more."

The King was delighted with the purse for he despised the giant. "Molly Whuppie," he said "you're a brave, bold girl and have done very well. If you would do better still, go back again and take the ring from the giant's finger, and I will marry you to my youngest son." Molly thought this would be good fortune indeed, so she agreed to try.

Once again she returned to the giant's house, where she hid and waited as before. When he was snoring loudly, she slipped out from beneath the bed and pulled at the ring on his finger. But the ring was tight. She pulled and pulled. At last it came off, but right at that moment the giant woke up and grabbed her. "Molly Whuppie," he roared, "if I'd done as much harm to you as you have done to me, what would you do to me?" he asked.

"Well," said Molly, "I'd put you in a sack with a dog and a cat and a needle and thread and shears. And I'd hang the whole lot of you from a hook. Then I'd go off into the woods and look for the biggest stick that I could find. Then I'd come back and bash the sack until you were dead!"

"Then," said the giant, "that's just what I'll do to you."

So he put her in a sack with a dog and a cat and a needle and thread and shears and he hung the whole lot of them from a hook. Then he went off to the woods to fetch the biggest stick that he could find.

Meanwhile, from inside the sack, Molly called out to the giant's wife, "Oh, if only you could see what I can see!"

"Why what do you see, Molly Whuppie?" his wife replied.

"Oh, if only you could see what I can see!" she called again.

"Why, what do you see, Molly Whuppie?" his wife replied.

"Oh, if only you could see what I can see," she called for a third time.

"Let me up," said the giant's wife, "so I can see it too."

Molly took the shears and cut a hole in the sack, big enough for her to climb out, then she helped the giant's wife to climb in. "Why, I can't see a thing in here, Molly." she said. "Help me down." But Molly had already set to work with the needle and thread. She stitched and stitched as quickly as she could, until the giant's wife was sewn up inside the sack.

The giant was coming back with a great stick so Molly hid behind the open door. He came in and whacked at the sack, he biffed it and bashed it and thwacked at the sack. The dog and the cat made such a noise that he could not hear his wife objecting. But he did see Molly creep out of the door and run.

He was after her at once. And again they ran and ran to the start of the Hair's Breadth Bridge. Molly got across but the giant could not follow. He stood and shook his fist in fury. "Molly Whuppie, oh, Molly Whuppie!" he roared until the ground shook beneath their feet. "Woe betide you, if you ever, ever come back here again."

"Oh, how you scare me! I wouldn't dare, ever come back again!" she cried from the other side.

The King was delighted with the ring for he loathed the giant. "Molly Whuppie," he said, "you're a brave, bold girl and have done very well. Indeed, you could not do better!" And it was true, for each wood-cutter's daughter married a prince. Which was very good fortune indeed.

Little Red Riding Hood

There was once a pretty little girl who was loved by everyone, especially her grandmother. And because her grandmother had made her a little red cape and hood she was known by one and all as Little Red Riding Hood.

One day her mother called her and said "Little Red Riding Hood, your grandma has been rather ill. I've made up a basket of good things and want you to take them to her. Seeing you will make her feel much better."

So Little Red Riding Hood took the basket and set out for Grandma's house which was on the other side of a wood. The day was fine and warm. Little Red Riding Hood skipped along the woodland path. Suddenly a wolf stepped out in front of her. He wanted to eat her on the spot because he was *so* hungry. But he had seen a wood-cutter close by, and he did not dare. So he said, "Little Red Riding Hood, where are you going with that basket of good things to eat?" And because she did not know how unwise it was to talk to wolves, she replied "Why, I'm taking it to Grandma's house. She's not been well, you know."

"Tut! Tut!" said the wolf, "What a shame! Where does she live? I might drop by and see her myself."

So the little girl pointed the way. "Goodbye then, Little Red Riding Hood." And then, as if by way of an after-thought, he added, "Why not pick her some flowers as well, I'm sure she'd like that very much." Then he hurried off down the path to be certain that it was he who got to the house first.

Little Red Riding Hood took her time. She played with the butterflies and birds and gathered up a great, big bunch of

flowers. In the meantime the wolf had arrived at Grandma's house.

He knocked at the door. A-rat-ta-tap-tap! "Who's there?" called the old lady. "It's me," said the wolf in his softest voice, "Little Red Riding Hood, with a basket of good things to eat, Grandma."

"Well, lift up the latch and come in, my dear." So he did and he swallowed Grandma up in one big gulp, because he was *so* hungry. Then he put on a nightgown, and her shawl and bonnet and hopped into bed.

Before long, there was another knock at the door. A-rat-ta-tap-tap! "Who's there?" called the wolf, in his softest voice. "Little Red Riding Hood, Grandma. I've brought you a basket of good things to eat."

"Well, lift up the latch and come in, my dear." Little Red Riding Hood did.

The wolf said "Come over here, close to the bed." Little Red Riding Hood was somewhat alarmed. Grandma did not look quite like Grandma should. She said, "Oh Grandma, what big eyes you have got!"

"All the better to see you with!" said the wolf.

She said, "Oh Grandma, what big ears you have got!"

"All the better to hear you with!" said the wolf.

She said, "Oh! Grandma, what big teeth you have got!"

"All the better to eat you with!" said the wolf. And with that he sprang up and swallowed Little Red Riding Hood down, in one great gulp because he was *so* hungry!

After having such a good meal, of Grandma and little girl, he felt rather tired and was soon fast asleep. He began to snore. He snored and he snored until the windows of the little house rattled.

Now the wood-cutter, who had finished his day's work was on his way home. He heard the wolf snoring and thought, "Grandma doesn't sound too well at all. I'd better stop and see if the old lady is all right." He knocked at the door. A-rat-ta-tap-tap! The wolf made no reply. So the wood-cutter lifted the latch and went in. He knew at once what had happened when he saw who was sleeping in Grandma's bed. He lifted his axe and chopped the wolf up, into two clean halves. From one half jumped little Red Riding Hood, from the other jumped Grandma, who was a wee bit shaken and a wee bit cross, but otherwise quite unharmed!

The Gingerbread Man

There was once an old couple who lived all by themselves, and they felt lonely. One day the little old lady said to her husband, "Little old man, I've had a good idea. I shall bake us a gingerbread man. He'll keep us company."

So that is what she did. She shaped the boy nicely out of gingerbread dough and gave him one currant for his mouth, two currants for eyes and three currants for the buttons down his front. He had a very mischievous look, and the couple were very pleased with him.

They placed him on a tray and put him in the oven to bake.

As soon as he was done, the little old lady opened the door and took him out. She had scarcely put the tray down on the table, when up the gingerbread man got and away he jumped, off the table and out of the house, singing:

"Run, run, as fast as you can, you can't catch me,
I'm the gingerbread man!"

And the couple could not.

The gingerbread man ran down the street. A horse saw him coming and thought he would be good to eat. "Stop, gingerbread man," he neighed. But the gingerbread man hopped out of reach, singing:

"Run, run, as fast as you can, you can't catch me,
I'm the gingerbread man!"

The horse could not.

He kept on running till he met a cow in a field. The cow saw him coming and thought he would be good to eat. "Stop, little gingerbread man," she mooed. But the gingerbread man skipped out of reach, singing:

"Run, run, as fast as you can, you can't catch me,
I'm the gingerbread man!"

The cow could not.

He kept on running till he met a farmer in his yard. The farmer saw him coming and thought he would be good to eat. "Stop little gingerbread man," he cried. But the gingerbread man jumped out of reach, singing:

"Run, run, as fast as you can, you can't catch me,
I'm the gingerbread man!"

The farmer could not.

The little gingerbread man kept on running but, at last, he came to a stream and had to stop. The little old couple, the horse, cow and farmer were not far behind. He was wondering what to do, when a fox stepped out of the bushes, close by. He had seen the little man coming, and thought he would be good to eat. He said, "Gingerbread man, if you hop onto my tail, I will carry you across the stream."

The gingerbread man hopped onto the fox's tail. The water was getting deep and the fox said, "Gingerbread man, skip onto my back and your feet will not get wet." The little gingerbread man skipped onto his back but the water was getting deeper and the fox said, "Gingerbread man, jump onto my nose and your feet will stay dry." So the little gingerbread man jumped onto his nose. The fox tossed him in the air and caught him with his mouth. He took a bite.

"Oh! dear," said the gingerbread man, "I am half gone!"

The fox took another bite.

"Oh! dear," said the gingerbread man, "I'm three quarters gone."

Then the fox took another bite, and the gingerbread man said nothing at all!

✦ Puss in Boots ✦

There was once a miller who had three sons. All he had to leave them when he died was his mill, a donkey and a cat. So the eldest one took the mill, the second the donkey, and the third, the cat.

The youngest son was dejected. "It's alright for the other two," he thought, "with the mill and the donkey together, they can earn a living. But what on earth can I do with an old cat? He was a good mouser in his day, but he'll hardly keep me from starving."

Now Puss, who was a very clever cat, knew just what his master was thinking and said, "Bring me a pair of boots and a large leather bag with drawstrings in it, and you will see that you haven't fared as badly as you think." The young man was surprised to hear the cat speak but did just what he was asked.

Puss was delighted with the boots. He pulled them on, picked up the bag and filled it with fresh, green leaves. He then strode off to a nearby field which he knew was teeming with rabbits. He laid the bag open and hid. Before long a young rabbit approached. It could not resist the leaves so it hopped into the open bag to feed.

Puss leant forward, pulled the strings firmly closed and with the rabbit caught inside the bag, went off to see the King.

"Your Majesty," said Puss, bowing low, "I bring you this gift from my Lord, the Marquis of Carabas."

"Oh, how kind!" said the King, for he loved rabbit. "Please convey my thanks to your master."

A day or two later, Puss pulled the same trick. This time he caught two fine, young partridge. And off he went again to see the King. "Oh, how kind!" said the King for he loved partridge. "Please convey my thanks to your master, the Marquis."

Puss carried on this way for several months. One day he heard that the King and his daughter were to take the air along a nearby river. He said to his master, "Do as I now tell you and your fortune will be made. Take off your clothes and wash yourself in the river." So the miller's youngest son did just as he was told. Meanwhile the cat hid his master's old clothes beneath a rock.

It was not long before the King's carriage came into view. Puss leapt out in front of it, waving his paws, shouting, "Help! Help! My Lord, the Marquis of Carabas is drowning!" The King commanded the carriage to stop and ordered his men to go at once to the aid of the Marquis, for he had proved to be a most loyal and generous subject.

That cunning old cat then told the King how thieves had stolen his master's clothes whilst he was bathing. The King was horrified and at once ordered that a suit of the very finest cloth should be fetched from his own wardrobe, for his friend, the Marquis.

How fine the miller's son looked, fresh from the water and dressed like a nobleman. The King insisted they should continue the drive together. Once inside the coach the King's daughter looked at the Marquis, and she thought him very handsome. The Marquis looked at the Princess and thought her very beautiful.

Puss was pleased. His plan was working well. He trotted along ahead of the coach. Soon he met some mowers in the meadow. He stopped and said, "Friends, the King is about to pass. If you do not tell him that this meadow belongs to the Marquis of Carabas, your heads will be cut off and chopped up as fine as parsley for the pot."

Shortly after the King's coach pulled up beside them. When the King asked to whom the fine meadow belonged, they bowed and said, "To our Lord, the Marquis of Carabas." For they were all afraid of losing their heads.

Puss still trotted on ahead. He came to a field of fine corn and he called to the reapers, "Friends! The King is about to pass. If you do not say that this corn you cut belongs to the Marquis of Carabas, you will have your heads cut off and chopped up as fine as parsley for the pot."

Soon the King's coach pulled up beside them. When the King asked to whom all the corn belonged they answered, "To our Lord, the Marquis of Carabas!" For they were all afraid as well.

Puss still kept ahead of the coach and said the same thing to all those he met on the way. The King was, by now, very impressed by the Marquis and the wonderful estates he owned.

At last Puss arrived at the grandest of castles. Now this castle and all the lands the Royal party had crossed belonged to a terrible Ogre. But Puss was clever and knew all there was to know about him. He asked for an audience and the Ogre received him. "I hear," said Puss, "that you have the power to change your form into anything you wish - an elephant or a lion for example."

"Of course!" replied the Ogre and to prove it he instantly transformed himself into a roaring lion. Puss was so startled that he ran up a pillar and onto a beam, which was not easy for a cat wearing boots! "A large animal is one thing," said Puss above the

Ogre's head, "but I have heard that you can turn yourself into tiny creatures too. Could you, for example, change into a mouse?"

"Of course!" replied the Ogre, as he changed from roaring lion to tiny squeaking mouse. Puss leapt down from the beam at once, pounced on the mouse and ate it up.

Meanwhile the King had seen the castle and decided to call on its owner. The cat heard the coach approach and ran out to meet them saying, "Welcome, Your Majesty, to the home of my Lord, the Marquis of Carabas."

"What!" exclaimed the King to the miller's son, "Does this magnificent castle also belong to you? How wonderful. Let's go inside, at once!"

They wined and they dined and they made very merry. The King was so pleased he soon suggested that the Marquis would make just the right husband for his beautiful daughter, and that they should marry without delay.

The couple were happy and so too was Puss, the old mill cat, who lived like a lord for the rest of his days, and never had to catch a mouse again, unless, of course, he wanted to.

The Three
Little Pigs

Have you ever heard the story of the three little pigs? As soon as they were old enough to look after themselves their mother said, "It's time to leave the farmyard and set up home for yourselves." So they packed up their belongings and set off down the lane.

They had not gone very far when they met a man who was carrying a load of straw. The first little pig piped up, "Please, man, give me that straw so that I can build myself a house." And the man did. The little pig was happy and built himself a house from it straight away, and went inside. He was very pleased with himself.

It was not very long before the wolf came to the straw house. He said, "Little pig, little pig, let me come in."

"Oh no, by the hairs on my chinny-chin-chin, I will not."

"Then I'll huff and I'll puff and I'll blow the house in," said the wolf.

So he huffed and he puffed and he blew the house in. And he ate the little pig right up.

Then there were only two little pigs walking down the lane. They had not gone much further when they met a man carrying a bundle of sticks. "Please, man, give me those sticks so that I can build myself a house." And the man did.

The second little pig built himself a house straight away. He went inside, very pleased with himself.

It was not very long before the wolf came by the stick house. He said, "Little pig, little pig, let me come in."

"Oh no, by the hairs on my chinny-chin-chin, I will not."

"Then I'll huff and I'll puff and I'll blow the house in."

So he huffed and he puffed and he puffed and he huffed and he blew the house in. Then he ate the little pig right up.

The third little pig was still walking down the lane when he met a man carrying a load of bricks. He said, "Please, man, give me those bricks so that I can build a house from them." And the man did.

So the third little pig set about building his house straight away. It was a good house and strong. The little pig went inside, very pleased with what he had done.

It was not very long before the wolf came by. He said, "Little pig, little pig, let me come in."

"Oh no, by the hairs on my chinny-chin-chin, I will not."

"Then I'll huff and I'll puff and I'll blow the house in." said the wolf. So he huffed and he puffed, he puffed and he huffed, but however much he blew, he could not blow the house in.

So he said, "Little pig, I know a field that's full of turnips."

"Where would that be?" said the little pig.

"It's in Farmer Smith's field, I'll take you there in the morning."

"At what time will you fetch me?" asked the pig.

"Six o'clock."

Well, the little pig made sure he was up at five o'clock. He went to the field and picked a big bunch of turnips. He was home again before the wolf came by to pick him up. Presently the wolf arrived. "Are you ready little pig?"

The little pig laughed and said, "Why, I've been there and back already, I'll have turnips for my dinner. They're cooking in the pot right now."

The wolf was very cross at having been tricked and he said, "Little pig, I know a tree which bears the finest apples in the world."

"Where's that?" asked the pig.

"Why, down at Merry Orchard. I'll take you there in the morning if you like."

"At what time?" asked the little pig.

"Five o'clock," said the wolf.

The little pig was up at four o'clock but this time he had farther to go. He was just climbing down from the tree, when he saw the wolf coming, so he said, "These apples are delicious, I'll throw one down for you." He threw the apple as far away as he could. While the wolf was running after it, the little pig jumped out of the tree and trotted off home as fast as his legs would carry him.

The wolf was very cross at having been tricked but he did not show it. The next day he went to the little pig's house and said, "There is a fair this afternoon, in the village over the hill. If you would like to go I'll come and fetch you."

"Oh yes!" said the little pig. "At what time?"

"Three o'clock," said the wolf.

The little pig left home at two o'clock. He went to the fair and bought a fine butter churn. He was just coming down the hill with it when he saw the wolf coming up the hill towards him. The little pig was frightened and did not know what to do. So he jumped into the butter churn to hide. But the churn began to roll. It rolled over and over and off down the hill knocking the wolf off his feet. Well the wolf was so scared that instead of going to the fair, he ran off home.

The next day he called round to tell the little pig about the awful roly-poly thing that knocked him over and frightened him so much that he had to go straight home.

The little pig laughed, "You mean, it was I who scared you? I'd been to the fair

where I bought a butter churn. I was just carrying it home when I saw you, coming up the hill towards me. I did not know what to do. So I jumped into the butter churn, and off it went! It was me inside that roly-poly thing!"

The wolf was very, very angry when he heard this. He climbed onto the roof of the little pig's house. "I'm going to eat you up!" he said. But the little pig knew just what to do. As the wolf was climbing down the chimney, the little pig put a large pot of water on the stove to boil. The little pig listened and at just the right moment he took the lid off the pot and the wolf fell in. So the little pig ate the wolf for his dinner!

The Frog Prince

In a woodland glade, beneath a willow tree, was a deep, deep well. And here, one afternoon, a princess came to play. She carried with her her favourite toy - a little golden ball. She tossed it into the air, without a care, over and over again, but, at last, it fell and rolled across the moss into the well.

The princess peered over the edge, but the ball sank to the bottom. She felt so sad she began to cry. "I'd give my finest clothes, my jewels and all that I own in the world to have that little golden ball back again." Her tears fell splish-splash into the well.

Just then a frog popped its head out of the water and said, "Pretty princess, I can get that little ball for you, but I do not want your fortune, clothes, nor jewels. Only this: You must take me home and love me, let me eat from your golden plate and sleep beside you on your pillow overnight." The princess agreed but secretly she thought, "What a fool this horrid frog is. As if I'd agree to such a thing!"

The frog disappeared beneath the water. After a while he came back with the ball in his mouth. As soon as the princess had it in her hand, she was off, leaving the poor frog behind. "Princess," he called, "a promise is a promise!" But she was already out of ear-shot, far away.

That evening she sat down to dinner with her family, and was about to eat, when she heard something tapping at the door. Someone outside it said,

"Pretty Princess, remember, please,
The promises you made,
To your true love, by the well,
Beneath the willow in the glade."

The princess opened the door. As soon as she saw the frog sitting outside she slammed it shut again. Her face was white with fear. The King and Queen were worried and asked her to explain. So she told them all about the frog and the well and the little golden ball. "I never thought he would. I never thought he even could climb out of the well and follow me."

Her father was stern. "A promise is a promise! Let him in!"

So the trembling girl obeyed. The frog hopped up beside her and said, "Lift me up and let me eat from your golden plate."

The princess did as she was told, and the frog said, "Now I have eaten I am tired. Take me up to your bedroom. Put me on the pillow where you lay your head." So the princess picked him up and carried him to her bedroom, where she had to sleep the whole night through beside the frog.

In the morning he hopped off the bed, down the stairs and was gone. "Thank goodness," thought the princess, "that's the last we'll see of him." But it was not to be, for the same thing happened on the next night and the next.

However, when she woke on the third morning, the frog was gone, but there beside the bed stood the most handsome young man she had ever seen. "Pretty princess," he said, "I was that horrid frog who frightened you." Then he told her how he was really a prince, that a witch had put a spell on him and changed his form, and how he had been forced to wait in the well beneath the willow tree until a princess came to break the spell. She had to let him eat from her plate and sleep on the bed beside her for three nights. Now the enchantment was lifted, he was free.

Well, the princess had fallen under a spell of her own. She was in love. So when the handsome prince proposed that he should take her to his father's kingdom, where they should marry, she was quick to agree. And before very long a magnificent coach arrived. It was drawn by white horses with plumes of feathers fluttering on their heads. They set off to the prince's home, where they lived happily for the rest of their days.

The Animal Band

There was once an old donkey. He had worked hard for years, carrying heavy loads of corn. Now his back was weak and his knees wobbled, his master did not want him any more. So fearing the worst the donkey left home, saying to himself, "When I bray I make a sound as good as any trumpet player I have heard. If they can earn a living, so can I."

He set off for town to try his luck. But a short way along the road he found a lame old dog, who was looking very glum and down in the mouth. "Why the long face, sir?" he inquired.

"My master's thrown me out. After all those years of faithful service too. Now I'm old and lame I can't help him hunt. Oh, what am I to do?"

"Don't despair, my friend. I've heard how dogs can bark and howl at the moon. I never heard a more melodious tune. Come along with me. Wandering minstrels we shall be. Two voices are better than one."

They went on together. Shortly, they met a very sorry looking cat. "What's up with you?" inquired the donkey, "You've a face like a wet, rainy day!"

"All my life I served my mistress, killing the rats and mice that eat her corn. But now I'm old and my teeth are worn away to stumps, she says I'm good for nothing. I must go. Oh, what am I to do?"

"Don't despair, madam," said the donkey, "we all know how you can yowl on the roof tops in the middle of the night. And a very fine song it is you sing. Come with us. Wandering minstrels we will be; great musicians. You shall see. Three voices are better than two."

So cat, dog and donkey went on together. They had not gone too far before they came to a farmyard. There on the gate post stood a cockerel. He was crowing at the top of his voice. "What's up with you?" inquired the donkey. "This is not the time of day you usually sing."

"I rise at dawn each morning to announce to one and all that it is time to leave their beds and start the day. But I overheard my Mistress say that she's expecting guests tomorrow and I'M TO BE THE DINNER! So I thought I'd have a crow, for all I'm worth, while I still could!"

"Don't despair, sir," said the donkey. "You are the very maestro of song. No one can hold a note like you. Come along with us and join our band. We'll make the finest choir in the land."

Cockerel, cat, dog and donkey carried on together towards the town. But dusk was falling and the animals decided they should pass the night in a nearby wood. The dog and the donkey lay down beneath a tree, while the cat jumped up into the branches and the cockerel flew to the very top. Now cockerels have keen eyes and from the top of the tree he spied a light. He called down to his friends, "We might be better off over there, where there's a house. We might find a scrap or two to eat."

So the animals made their way towards the light. The donkey went to the window. There he saw a table laid out for a feast. Around it sat a band of robbers, surrounded by their gold. They were eating and drinking and enjoying themselves.

"Well," said the donkey, "that'll do for me." He told his friends what he had seen. They all got together and decided what to do. If they wanted the feast, they must scare the robbers off.

The dog was to jump onto the donkey's back, the cat was to scramble onto the dog's and the cockerel was to fly up and perch

on the cat. Then they should all sing out together at the top of their voices.

So the dog jumped onto the donkey, the cat onto the dog and the cockerel flew up and perched on the cat. Then in one fearful blast, donkey brayed, dog barked, cat yowled and cockerel crew. They charged at the window and the donkey smashed the glass with his hooves. The terrified robbers dropped their food and ran out of the house and away into the woods.

The animals made themselves at home and tucked into the feast. Then they settled down to sleep, the cat beside the dying fire where it was warm, the dog by the door, the donkey in the yard and the cock up on the roof.

When all was quiet and dark, one of the robbers returned. He crept into the dark house. The only thing he saw were the eyes of the cat, glinting in the corner where the fire had been. Mistaking them for embers, he took a taper from his pocket and stuck it in her face to get a light. The cat hissed and scratched him. The man jumped back. The dog leapt forward and bit him on the leg. As the man made his escape, the donkey gave him a kick in the back and from the top of the roof, the cockerel crew "Cock-a-doodle-do!"

The robber was so scared when he reached his companions. He said, "That place is full of demons, I'll never go back, never, not for all the gold in the world. I was spat at and scratched by a witch at the fire. There was a devil by the door who stabbed me in the leg and a demon in the yard, who hit me in the back with a club and as if that was not enough, there was another, on the roof top calling his companions to 'Get a chopper too!'"

Robbers or not, not one of them dared ever go back.

As for the animal band, they became quite well known. They made music for country folk and fared very well. And they all lived together undisturbed, in their cosy little house in the woods.

The Three Bears

Daddy Bear, Mummy Bear and Baby Bear lived in a cosy cottage in the woods. One day they made porridge for their breakfast and they put it into three bowls: a great big bowl for Daddy Bear, a medium-sized bowl for Mummy Bear and a tiny little bowl for Baby Bear. It was far too hot to eat so they went for a walk while it cooled off.

Now it happened that a girl, whose name was Goldilocks because she had long golden hair, was passing the cottage and smelt breakfast. She went to the door and knocked. When there came no reply she peeped in at the windows. She saw that no one was home and because she was rather naughty she just walked in. It was not a polite thing to do!

There on the table she saw the bowls of porridge. It looked so good she just had to try some. First she tasted the porridge in the great big bowl. It was too hot. Then she tasted the porridge in the medium-sized bowl. It was too cold. Then she tasted the porridge in the tiny little bowl. It was not too hot and it was not too cold. It was just right, and she ate it all up!

Then she thought she would like to sit down, so she looked around and saw three chairs. First she sat down on the great big

chair, but it was too hard. Then she sat down on the medium-sized chair, but it was too soft. Then she sat down on the tiny little chair. It was not too hard and it was not too soft. It was just right, but Goldilocks was too big and she broke it!

Then she thought she would like to lie down, so she looked around and saw three beds. First she lay down on the great big bed, but it was too high. Then she lay down on the medium-sized bed, but it was too low. Then she lay down on the tiny little bed.

It was just right. She was so comfortable she dropped off to sleep.

Now, thinking that the porridge would be ready to eat, the three bears returned from their walk. When Daddy Bear looked at his great, big bowl, he saw that his spoon had been left standing up in it, and he said, "Someone's been eating MY porridge!" When Mummy Bear looked at her medium-sized bowl and saw that the spoon had been left standing up in it, she said, "Someone's been eating MY porridge!" But when Baby Bear looked at his tiny little bowl, he burst into tears and cried, "Someone's been eating MY porridge and they've eaten it all up!"

The bears were worried. They looked around and when Daddy Bear saw that the cushion on his great big chair was out of place, he said, "Someone's been sitting in MY chair!" When Mummy Bear looked at her medium-sized chair and saw that the cushion was out of place, she said, "Someone's been sitting in MY chair!" But when Baby Bear looked at his tiny little chair, he burst into tears and cried, "Someone's been sitting in MY chair and they've broken it!"

The bears were very worried. So they looked around some more. Then Daddy Bear noticed that the pillow on his great big bed had been disturbed and said, "Someone's been lying on MY bed." Then Mummy Bear looked at her medium-sized bed and noticed that her pillow had been disturbed, and said, "Someone's been lying on MY bed." Then Baby Bear looked at his tiny little bed and cried out, "Someone's been lying on MY bed and she's still here!"

"WHO IS SHE?!" shouted the three bears all together. Startled by this noise, Goldilocks woke up. When she saw the bears crowded round her, she was very frightened. She leapt out of bed and jumped through a window and ran away into the wood, and the three bears were never troubled by that bad little girl, ever again.

The Twelve
Dancing Princesses

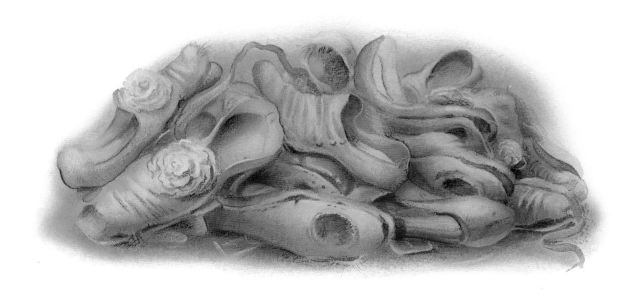

If you needed a new pair of shoes every day, your parents would not be pleased. Shoes are not cheap; they never were. So you can imagine how annoyed the King was when he found he was having to have a new pair made for each of his twelve daughters every day. He came to the conclusion that the only way shoes could be worn out so quickly was by dancing.

He forbade it and locked the girls in their bedroom every night so that they could not go out. That would put an end to this dancing business. But every morning it was just the same - there lay a heap of shoes, all tattered and battered and full of holes.

It was costing him a fortune and he grew quite cross. "This will not do," he said. "If any man can discover where my daughters are going to dance, he shall marry whichever one he wishes and inherit my kingdom after my death. But if he has not solved the mystery after three whole days and nights," he said, "he will have his head chopped off."

Not long after, a young nobleman arrived to try his luck. He was given a seat in a little room, just to the side of the girls' bedroom. He was instructed to watch all night. He was determined to keep awake. But after one of the girls had offered him a glass of wine, his eyes began to shut and they did not open till the morning. By then it was too late, for there lay the shoes, all full of holes. The same thing happened on the second night and the third. And good as his word, and because he was so very cross, the King had the young man's head chopped off.

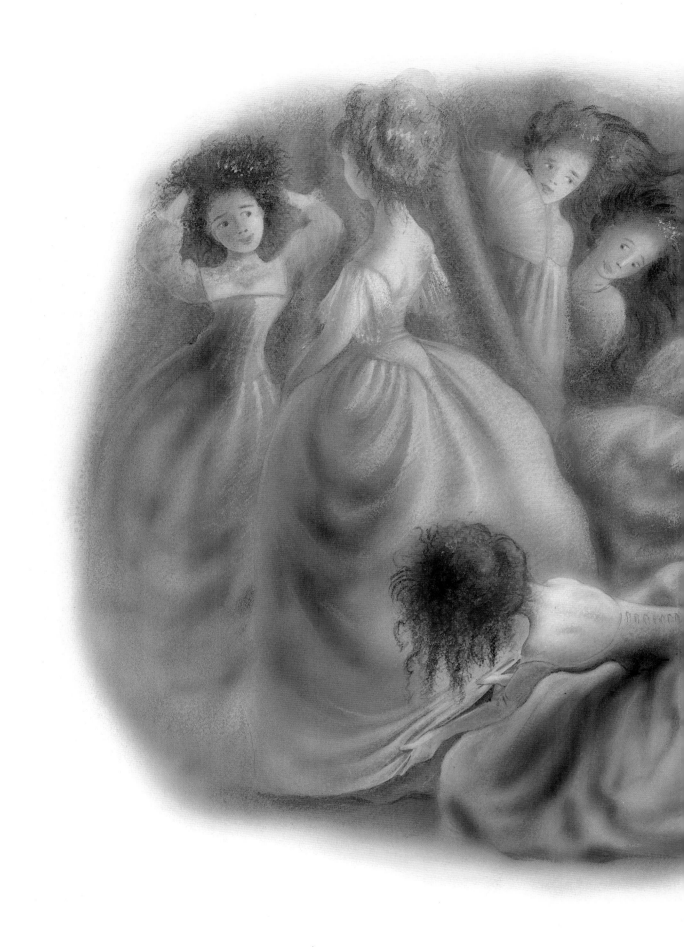

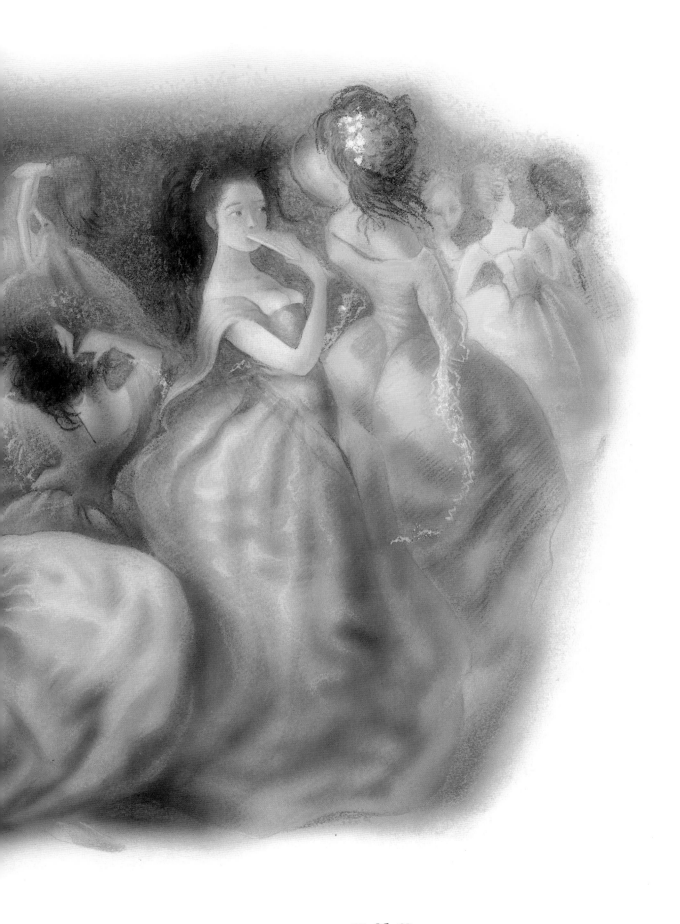

It did not seem too hard a challenge and as the rewards were high, word soon spread. So more and more young noblemen arrived to try their luck. Score by score, young noblemen arrived, yet the same fate befell them all.

Now it happened that a poor soldier, who had been wounded in a battle and could no longer fight, was wandering, lost and hungry, through a nearby wood when he met an old woman gathering sticks. He helped her with her work and they chatted for a while. She asked him where he was going.

"Oh!" said he in jest, "I thought I might go to the castle and see if I can solve the mystery of the twelve princesses. I might make my fortune. I might become King. I wouldn't be hungry then. But I might lose my head as well as my way," he said and laughed.

"Well," said the old woman, "be serious. You've helped me with my work, I'll help you with yours. Now listen hard. You must not drink the wine they offer. You must pretend to fall asleep. And you must take this little cloak. It'll make you quite invisible. And don't forget to gather proof." She handed him the cloak, pointed him in the right direction and disappeared.

The soldier was impressed. Armed with the cloak and good advice, he decided to have a go. The King was a little surprised to see such a poor and humble man come forward to accept the challenge. The chances were he would lose his head. But if he succeeded where so many had failed, why should he not marry a king's daughter?

So that night the soldier found himself sitting in the little room just as the others had done. It was not long before the eldest of the daughters came and offered him some wine. "Thank you," he said and put the glass up to his lips pretending to take a drink. Then he yawned and stretched and made out he was nodding off. As soon as she was gone he poured the wine away. Then he heard whispering and rustling, giggling and bustling. He guessed that, far from going to bed, they were dressing for something special.

The twelve girls came and looked at him. They found the soldier slumped in his chair, the wine glass fallen to the floor. "This one's well away," said one. "The glass is empty," said another, and they laughed, but the youngest one held back. "I feel uneasy tonight," she said. "Are you sure he's quite asleep? His eyes seem open just a peep."

"Oh, stop that, you scaredycat! He's snoring his head right off!" Then even the youngest began to laugh and they ran to the eldest sister's bed and rapped on one of the posts.

The bed began to move aside. Behind it was a hidden door and flight of steps down which they ran very fast, the eldest first, the youngest last, followed closely by the soldier, who had wrapped himself in his magic cloak. But half way down the stairs he trod on the youngest sister's hem. "Oh, someone's following us!" she cried, "I felt them pulling at my skirt."

"Oh, stop that, you scaredycat! Can't you see there's no one there? You caught your dress on a broken stair," called the others.

Then the stairs became an avenue of glistening silver trees through which the twelve princesses ran. The soldier broke off a twig and hid it beneath his little cloak. The youngest sister heard it snap. "Did you hear that?" she cried. "Someone's surely following us."

"Oh, stop that, you scaredycat! It was a gun fired to salute us," called the others as they hurried on.

The silver trees turned to gold. The soldier broke off another twig. The youngest sister heard it snap. "Did you hear that?" she cried.

"Oh, stop that, you scaredycat! It was a firework let off to welcome us," called the others and they hurried on.

The golden trees gave way to trees with leaves that shone with diamonds. The soldier broke off another twig. The youngest sister heard it crack. "Did you hear that?" she cried.

"Oh, stop that, you scaredycat! It was the sound of our patience snapping. Quickly now or we'll all be late." And the sisters hurried on until they reached the shores of a lake.

Twelve princes awaited them in twelve small boats, one for each princess. And the sisters jumped in. The soldier jumped in too, and sat beside the youngest, all unseen. "Oh!" said her prince, as he began to row, "this little boat seems heavy tonight. It's going to be hard work."

"Did you hear what he said?" she called to the others.

"Oh, stop that, you scaredycat, it's just because the night's so warm. Of course it's heavy going," was what her sisters replied, while their partners kept on rowing.

They came to an island in the middle of the lake. It was an enchanted place for sure. On it stood a palace hung with many coloured lights. Here wine flowed from fountains and wild music played. Once the sisters heard the strains they leapt in the air. They clapped their hands. They stamped their feet and they danced. The soldier danced with them too, all unseen.

Then something happened that scared the youngest more than anything had before. The dancers paused a while to drink. Wine was poured into the youngest sister's cup but before she could raise it to her mouth the soldier gulped it down.

"Did you see that?" she cried, "That goblet has just been filled but now the wine's all gone. I never had the chance to drink it. Whatever is going on?"

Though the other sisters noticed, they shrugged it off and sighed, "Oh, stop that, you scaredycat. Let's dance while we have the chance. It won't be long before it's dawn." Then they danced and danced and danced. They danced till their shoes were full of holes. They danced till the eastern sky grew light.

Then the music died down and the wine dried up and the palace faded clean away. And the princes rowed the sisters back across the lake together with the soldier, all unseen.

He ran along the avenues, up the stairs and across the room, flung his cloak into a corner and slumped down in his chair. He was snoring so loudly when the girls returned that even the youngest of them laughed. Then they kicked off their shoes, all full of holes, hung up their dresses and went to bed.

The same thing happened on the second night and the third. Only on this, the last night of the challenge, the soldier not only drank from the youngest sister's cup but took it away with him too.

The morning came and the King called for the soldier. The sisters hid outside the door to hear what he had to say before he lost his head, like all the others.

"Have you solved the mystery?" demanded the King.

"Indeed I have," replied the soldier. "They tried to drug me with a drink that makes a person sleep, but I drank not a drop. I made myself invisible and followed them down some secret stairs, along an avenue of silver trees and an avenue of gold and an avenue of trees whose leaves shone with diamonds. I followed them to a lake where twelve princes awaited them, in twelve little boats. They rowed them to an island where an enchanted palace stood, where wine flowed and music played and the princesses danced till dawn. They danced till their shoes were all worn out and the soles were full of holes."

The King, who was very angry, called for his daughters. They blushed and trembled and hung their heads. Then the eldest said, "How do you know he's telling the truth? Ask him if he has some proof!"

Then the soldier produced the silver twig and the golden twig and the twig whose leaves shone with diamonds and last of all the youngest sister's goblet.

So the challenge was completed, and the King was as good as his word. "Which of my daughters will you wed?"

"The oldest and the boldest," answered the soldier without hesitating, for he liked her courage. And so it was in time he inherited the kingdom. What happened to the princes, or their enchanted palace, I really cannot tell. But the secret stairs were sealed up, and the princesses no longer wore their shoes out faster than you or I.

Town Mouse, Country Mouse

There was once a mouse who lived in the country, feeding off grain and food that grew wild. His home was a hole by the edge of a wood. It was a very simple but contented life. Now the country mouse had a friend who lived in a great city. He invited the town mouse to come and stay. "It would be a treat for you," he said, "all that fresh air and plenty of good plain food."

The town mouse accepted and arrived for his holiday. The country mouse did all he could to see his friend was comfortable. He made him a bed of soft dry moss and he took him to the finest fields he knew, where peas and wheat and wholesome things grew.

But the town mouse was not happy. "How can you bear such a humble life? You sleep on moss, in a pokey hole, in a ditch by the edge of a wood. You have the poorest, most boring diet I know. And how you have to work to get it, all day long in an open field whatever the weather may bring. What do you do when it starts to rain? Or when the sun burns your back? Or when the snow comes down and covers the fields, where do you find your food then? It's not the life I'd choose."

"My home is quite dry and warm," said his friend. "It is adequate for me. In the summer when the days are long, I stock up so that when the hardest weather comes and the snow is deep, I can stay tucked up at home and sleep. And my diet's not so dull; I climb brambles for the berries, and all sorts of wild food grows along the hedges. In the autumn I've a feast for there are fallen nuts to gather, and fruits and shoots and roots to gnaw. There's always something to be done. I'm never bored and never hungry."

"That sounds like very hard work to me. I, for one, am going home. Come along too, and you will see, how gracious city life can be. There's chocolate and cheese and cake to eat, and there's fresh fruit and dried fruit and fruit from afar, and all the nuts a mouse could wish for, and oh, the bacon rind!" he added, "And you don't have to lift a paw. It's all right there, laid out and waiting."

This did indeed sound good. The country mouse wondered what he had been missing and agreed to go along.

After a long journey they arrived at a house in the middle of town. The town mouse showed his friend around. And because travelling had made them tired, he took him to his bedroom in the stuffing of a chair. "It's the finest horsehair in the land," said he. They were just getting comfy when someone sat down. It was such a squeeze they could hardly breathe.

They hauled themselves out and ran. But even when they reached the shelter of the shadows they could not relax, for the house was patrolled by wicked, watchful cats. They had to keep their wits about them all the time.

"You must be getting hungry," said the town mouse to the country mouse. "Let me show you what a city larder looks like."

It was true, the pantry was filled, just as he had described it. The country mouse was hungry and he couldn't wait to eat. But the house was full of noises and sounds he did not know and every time he reached for something a trap would snap, or a shadow pass, or the larder door would open and a maid come in.

"I hope you'll forgive me, friend," he said, "I'm just too anxious to eat. You've every dish that a mouse could wish for but you can't take your meals in peace. I'd rather go back to a humble life, feeding on simple food, than avoiding the cats and snapping traps and snatching a bite now and then. Your bed may be fine but I'd rather have mine. I'm going home to my quiet little hole, by the ditch at the edge of the wood."

And that is exactly what he did.

Rapunzel

A long time ago and in another country there lived a poor man and his wife. They occupied a small room which overlooked a high-walled garden. The woman, who had been very ill, stood at the window and looked down at the vegetables and herbs that grew there.

"I must have some. I must have some," she sighed, as she gazed with longing at some crisp, bright rampian. "I think I cannot live without some."

She was so thin and pale, her husband was certain she would die if she did not have her wish. So he promised to get her some. Now the problem was that the garden belonged to a witch whose name was Gothel. Everyone knew that and everyone was afraid of her. If he had not been so scared, he could have tapped on the window in the evening, when he saw her tending the plot, and asked for a plant or two. Surely, no neighbour would have refused such a request when they heard how ill his wife had been. But the poor soul was timid and truly frightened by the old witch. So he decided that as he dared not ask, he would climb in after dark and steal some.

That night, when the lights went out in the witch's windows, he crept out of his house and climbed over her wall. He had just pulled up a handful or two when a terrible voice behind him shrieked, "How dare you! How dare you! How dare you come climbing into my garden like a common thief. How dare you steal my rampian, you wicked, wicked man! You will be punished!"

The poor man was so terrified his knees shook, his heart thumped and his teeth chattered so much he could hardly speak. When he finally got some words out he said, "Forgive me. I did it for my wife. She is so frail and ill she will fade away if she doesn't eat this plant."

"All right," said the witch, calming down a little. "If it's to save her life, you may take what you wish. On one condition. When your wife has a baby, you must give that child to me." The poor man really had no choice, for without the rampian his wife would surely die. So he agreed.

Every day he took his wife a bunch or two, every day she grew a little fitter, every day she grew a little fatter until one day a baby was born to the couple. At once, Gothel came knocking at the door. "Give me the child." she cried, "We made a bargain. I kept my side; now you keep yours." The poor man did as he had promised, although it broke his heart. He handed the baby over to the witch.

Gothel called her Rapunzel, after the rampian her father had taken, for that was the name by which the plant was known in her country. The baby grew into a little girl with golden hair: hair that the witch would never cut. The little girl grew into a beautiful young woman, she was more than beautiful, she was wondrous, with the longest most lustrous hair you ever saw. Then Gothel became jealous. A girl that looked like this would not stay with her long. Some day soon a fine young man would come along and marry Rapunzel and the witch would be left on her own.

So she shut the girl away in a tower which stood in a clearing of a forest. It had neither door nor stairs. There was just a small room, right at the top which could only be entered by its little window. Gothel came to visit her every day and bring her food. She would stand beneath the tower and call "Rapunzel! Rapunzel! Let down your hair." And Rapunzel would lean out and let her golden hair come tumbling down. There were yards and yards of it. Then the witch would grasp the hair in her hands and pull herself slowly up and up the face of the tower and in through the window.

Life was so lonely for Rapunzel; all she could do to comfort herself was sing. Now she not only possessed the longest, most lustrous hair you ever saw, she also had the sweetest voice you have ever heard. And it happened one day, that a prince, riding through the forest, heard that voice and stopped to listen. It seemed to come from the top of the tower. He wanted to see who was singing and walked round and round the base, trying to find an entrance; but there was no door to be seen. He was so haunted by the voice that he came back again day after day to listen. Once he was standing in the shadow beneath a tree enjoying Rapunzel's song, when the witch came along. She stood at the foot of the tower and called "Rapunzel! Rapunzel! Let down your hair." And to his surprise he saw the golden tresses come tumbling down and down. He watched how Gothel climbed them.

"Ah!" he said to himself, "So that's how it's done. I shall try too."

After the witch had left, but before the sun went down, he too stood at the foot of the tower. "Rapunzel! Rapunzel! Let down your hair," he called.

Just as before, the hair came tumbling down and the prince climbed up and in at the window. Rapunzel was shocked to see a stranger in her room, for apart from the witch she never had visitors. But the prince assured her that he meant no harm and that he came as a friend. Before long the two had fallen in love and the prince asked if she would marry him. Rapunzel agreed. But there was a problem.

How could Rapunzel escape from the tower? She could not climb down her own hair. So she said, "Bring me a skein of silk every evening and I will weave a ladder from it. When the ladder is long enough we can climb down and run away." All would have been well, had Rapunzel not said to Gothel during one of her visits, "How is it Mother, that you are so heavy and slow when you climb my hair, while my prince is so light and fast?"

"What?" shrieked the witch, "What? You treacherous child! How you have deceived me. I brought you to this lonely place to keep you from the world. You have betrayed me. You don't deserve my love." Then she picked up a pair of scissors and snip, snap, cut off Rapunzel's hair. The witch picked up the hair and tied it to two hooks on the inside of the window.

Then she took Rapunzel to a desert and left her there to fend for herself. Gothel returned to the tower and waited for the prince to arrive. Before long she heard a voice below call, "Rapunzel!

Rapunzel! Let down your hair." Whereupon the golden tresses came tumbling down. The prince climbed up as usual. But in place of the beautiful Rapunzel he found the witch! Her face was dark as a thunderstorm.

"Your little bird has gone," she hissed. "You will never see her again. The cat that caught her will now catch you!" And she drew the scissors from behind her back, like a cat with her claws out, ready to pounce. In order to save himself, the prince leapt from the window. He plunged to the ground.

A bramble bush broke his fall and probably saved his life, but thorns stuck in his eyes and he was blinded. For days and days he staggered around lost and confused, unable to see, unable to eat, until one day he stumbled into the desert where Rapunzel had been abandoned. He fell on the ground exhausted and would probably have died right there, but in the distance someone was singing. He knew the voice so well.

"Rapunzel, oh Rapunzel!" he cried, summoning all his strength. Rapunzel stopped singing and listened hard. Someone was calling her. It was unmistakable. She heard him call again and followed the sound until she found where her prince lay.

The tears began to flow when she saw the terrible state he was in. They fell from her eyes into his. They fell and they fell until they washed away the thorns that had blinded him, and soon his sight returned. Then he knew at once where they were. He took her back to his home, and when his strength returned he married her. They were very, very happy.

But what became of that wicked old witch? When the prince had fallen from the window, so too had Rapunzel's hair. It lay caught in the brambles at the foot of the tower so Gothel could not climb down.

She was so hated and feared no one would help her. She is probably still there, at the top of the tower she had so cruelly and cunningly created; a tower without door nor stairs.